W9-AVX-622

54318

BUTTERFIELD SCHOOL LIBRARY
1441 W. Lake Street
Libertyville, Illinois 60048

DEMCO

This book was a
gift to the Butterfield
School Library to
honor the birthday of

Gretta Goldsberry

February 5, 2003

THE LOST TOOTH CLUB

Arden Johnson

Tricycle Press
Berkeley, California

To all The Lost Tooth Club members of the world.

Copyright © 1998 by Arden Johnson
All rights reserved. No part of this book may be reproduced in any form without the written permission of the publisher, except in the case of brief quotations embodied in critical articles or reviews.

TRICYCLE PRESS
P.O. Box 7123
Berkeley, California 94707

Library of Congress Cataloging-in-Publication Data
 Johnson, Arden.
   The Lost Tooth Club / Arden Johnson.
       p.   cm.
Summary: Olivia tries all sorts of tricky ways to get into the Lost Tooth Club when her loose tooth just won't fall out.
   ISBN 1-883672-55-4
   [1. Teeth—Fiction. 2. Clubs—Fiction.]   I. Title.
PZ7.P44723Lo 1998
[E]—dc21   97-29723
                                                                        CIP
                                                                        AC

Printed in Hong Kong
1 2 3 4 5 6 — 01 00 99 98 97

Olivia wanted to get into The Lost Tooth Club more than anything else in the world.

There was only one problem.
She hadn't lost a tooth, and it
seemed like she never would.

She *did* have a wiggly front tooth that she had been trying to lose for weeks. She bit into crisp apples, chewy pizza, corn on the cob. Nothing worked. The tooth stayed in her mouth.

Looking out her window, Olivia thought she saw the moon smiling with a missing tooth. She fell asleep to dreams of a polar bear with a missing tooth, a squirrel with a missing tooth, a mouse with a missing tooth, her cat, Ferdi, with a missing tooth, and her dog, Petey, with no front tooth.

And all of them were running over to her friend Alisa's house
to join The Lost Tooth Club.

Olivia woke up with a start. "No way," she said. "They can't join without me!" She leaped out of bed, threw on her clothes, and ran next door to the clubhouse.

Olivia said to Alisa, "My tooth is pointing so far out that I can stick my tongue almost all the way through and pretend there's an empty spot. Doesn't that count?"

Alisa crossed her arms. "A tooth isn't lost until it's lost." She shut the clubhouse door.

Olivia could hear Matt, Sophie, Alisa, and the others planning
The Lost Tooth Club soft food party. She wanted to eat colored
mashed potatoes and chocolate pudding, too. She knew they
were wearing their Lost Tooth Club badges. She wanted a badge
like that.

Olivia ran back to her house and found one of her black markers. She colored her loose tooth black and looked in the mirror. It looked pretty good, just like it wasn't there.

BUTTERFIELD
1441 W. ———
Libertyville, Illinois ————

Olivia ran back to the clubhouse and yelled, "It happened, guys! Finally, it happened!" The door opened and they all crowded out to see.

"My tooth, it's fallen out, look!" Olivia hollered.

"Whoa," said Sophie. "Let's see." Olivia smiled what she thought was a big gappy smile, but the marker had come off. Her tooth still wiggled away.

The Lost Tooth Club members all chanted, "You still have all your teeth. You can't join the club yet!" Olivia walked slowly back to her yard. Even there she could still hear them giggling.

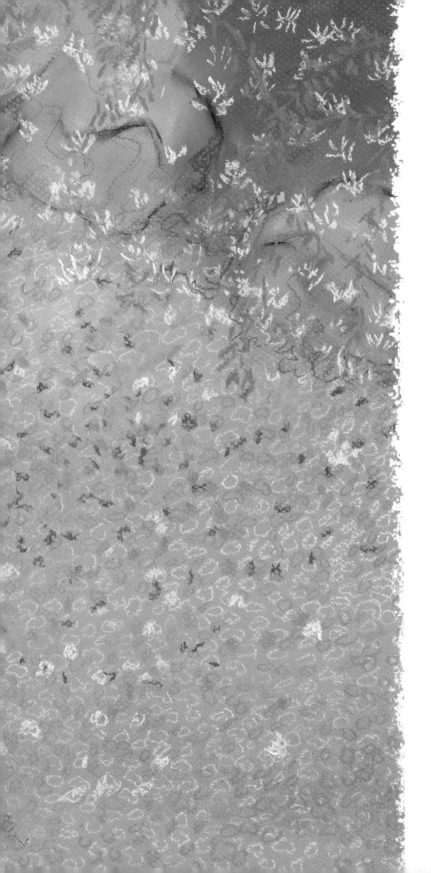

"Petey, I have an idea," said Olivia. She grabbed a piece of black licorice and pushed it onto her tooth. "Looks like an empty spot to me," she told her face in the mirror. Olivia ran to her driveway and found a little white pebble. "This looks just like a tooth!"

Off she crawled under the bushes to Alisa's house, shouting, "It's happened! All right! It's out! I've lost that tooth!"

Olivia handed Alisa the pebble. But just when Sophie was about to say congratulations, the piece of licorice fell off. Alisa shook her head and everyone laughed.

"That was a good one, Olivia," said Matt.

Once again, Olivia shuffled back to her own yard. She climbed to her favorite place and wiggled her tooth back and forth, and side to side, as hard as she could. "Ouch! Petey, it will be the day the dinosaurs come back when this tooth falls out," she said.

From where she sat Olivia could hear The Lost Tooth Club members talking.

"Olivia is so tricky," said Chris. Alisa and Matt were drawing pictures of how they lost their first teeth.

Sophie was saying to Alisa, "I can't believe you lost yours by diving into the pool. Nice picture! That will look great in the Lost Tooth album."

That was more than Olivia could take. She stormed back to the clubhouse, shouting, "That's it, I don't need you! I've had it! I don't care if I ever get into your club!" All the kids looked out the window to see Olivia stomp and shout. "I'll start The *Loose* Tooth Club and I'll be the President! I will have loose baby teeth for the rest of my life! I'll have a big mouth with teeny tiny loose teeth!"

Olivia spun around to leave.
"Come on, Petey, let's go!
Where are you? Come on, boy,
let's go, now! Ow!"

Out flew her tooth.

Alisa, Sophie, and Matt ran from the window and opened the door.

Alisa stared, then grinned her gappy grin. "Welcome to The Lost Tooth Club!"

Everyone gathered to admire the tooth and the nice new wide space in Olivia's mouth. They couldn't wait to see the special picture she would draw of how she lost her first tooth.

Dear Reader,

I'd love to hear about how you lost your tooth. If you draw a picture or write a story about it, I'll send you an official Lost Tooth Club badge. Send your drawings or stories to:

Lost Tooth Club
c/o Tricycle Press
P.O. Box 7123
Berkeley, CA 94707

I can't wait to find out how you lost your tooth!

Arden Johnson

P.S. Sorry, I can't return what you send me.